ELMER

David McKee

Andersen Press

D0185553

There was once a herd of elephants. Elephants young, elephants old, elephants tall or fat or thin. Elephants like this, that or the other, all different but all happy and all the same colour. All, that is, except Elmer.

Elmer was different. Elmer was patchwork.
Elmer was yellow and orange
and red and pink and purple
and blue and green
and black and white.

Elmer was *not* elephant colour.

It was Elmer who kept the elephants happy. Sometimes he joked with the other elephants, sometimes they joked with him. But if there was even a little smile, it was usually Elmer who started it.

One night Elmer couldn't sleep for thinking, and the think that he was thinking was that he was tired of being different. "Whoever heard of a patchwork elephant?" he thought. "No wonder they laugh at me."

In the morning before the others were really awake, Elmer slipped quietly away, unnoticed.

As he walked through the jungle, Elmer met other animals.

They always said: "Good morning, Elmer." Each time,
Elmer smiled and said: "Good morning."

After a long walk, Elmer found what he was looking for – a large bush. A large bush covered with berries, a large bush covered with elephant-coloured berries. Elmer caught hold of the bush and shook it and shook it so that the berries fell on the ground.

Once the ground was covered in berries, Elmer lay down and rolled over and over – this way and that way and back again. Then he picked up bunches of berries and rubbed himself all over, covering himself with berry juice until there wasn't a sign of any yellow, or orange, or red, or pink, or purple, or blue, or green, or black, or white.

When he had finished, Elmer looked like any other elephant.

After that Elmer set off back to the herd.
On the way, he passed the other animals again.

This time each one said to him: "Good morning,
elephant." And each time Elmer smiled and said:
"Good morning," pleased that he wasn't recognised.

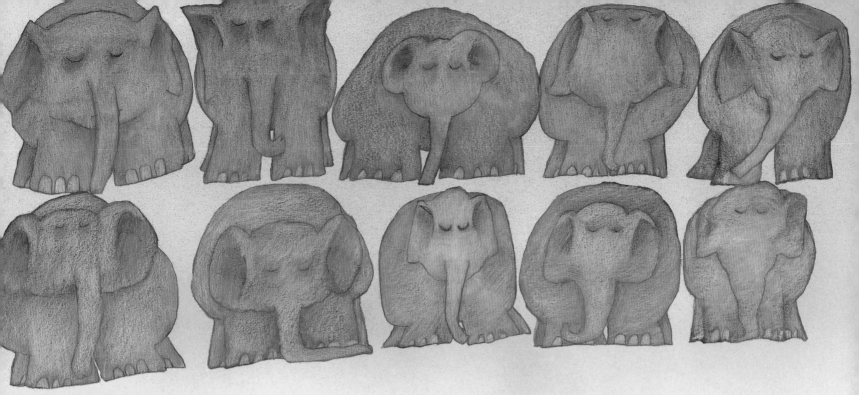

When Elmer rejoined the other elephants, they were all standing quietly. None of them noticed Elmer as he worked his way to the middle of the herd.

After a while Elmer felt that something was wrong. But what? He looked around: same old jungle, same old bright sky, same old rain cloud that came over from time to time and lastly same old elephants. Elmer looked at them.

The elephants were standing absolutely still.
Elmer had never seen them so serious before.
The more he looked at the serious, silent, still,

standing elephants, the more he wanted to laugh.
Finally he could bear it no longer.
He lifted his trunk and at the top of his voice shouted:

The elephants jumped and fell all ways in surprise.
"Oh my gosh and golly!" they said –
and then saw Elmer, helpless with laughter.

"Elmer," they said. "It must be Elmer."
Then the other elephants laughed too, as they had never laughed before.

As they laughed, the rain cloud burst and when the rain fell on Elmer, his patchwork started to show again. The elephants still laughed as Elmer was washed back to normal. "Oh Elmer," gasped an old elephant. "You've played some good jokes, but this has been the

biggest laugh of all. It didn't take you long to show
your true colours."
"We must celebrate this day every year," said another.
"This will be Elmer's Day. All elephants must decorate
themselves and Elmer will decorate himself elephant colour."

That is exactly what the elephants do.
On one day a year they decorate themselves and parade.
On that day if you happen to see an elephant ordinary
elephant colour, you will know it must be Elmer.

for Brett

First published in Great Britain in 1989 by Andersen Press Ltd.,
20 Vauxhall Bridge Road, London SW1V 2SA.
Copyright © David McKee, 1989.
The right of David McKee to be identified as the author and
illustrator of this work has been asserted by him in accordance
with the Copyright, Designs and Patents Act, 1988.
All rights reserved.
Printed and bound in Malaysia.
11   13   15   17   20   18   16   14   12
British Library Cataloguing in Publication Data available.
ISBN 978 1 84270 731 9